Gu

KIANGSI
FUKIEN
116
Chiao-ling
P'ing-yüan
Mei Chiang
Ho-p'ing
(Yang-ming)
Mei-hsien
Ta-pu
(Hu-liao)
MEI-HSIEN
C. C.
Lung-ch'uan
(Lao-lung)
Hsing-ning
Han Chiang
24
ung Chiang
Wu-hua
(Shui-chai)
Feng-shun
FUKIEN
Jao-p'ing
Ch'ao-an
an
Tzu-chin
Chieh-yang
C. C.
Ch'eng-hai
Nan-ao
Chieh-hsi
(Ho-p'o)
SWATOW
(SHAN-T'OU)
P'u-ning
Ch'ao-yang
SHAN-T'OU C. C.
Hui-lai
Hai-feng
Lu-feng

Chinese Fairy Tales

by Adele M. Fielde

Edited by Malcolm and Margaret Rosholt

First Edition

With best wishes
to
Don McCormick
from [illegible]
Feb 22, 2002
You [illegible] [illegible], Indeed

Library of Congress Catalog Card Number:
98-68105

ISBN 0-910417-11-3

Rosholt House
406 River Drive
Rosholt, Wisconsin 54473
(715) 677-4722

Printed in the United States of America by
Palmer Publications, Inc., Amherst, Wisconsin 54406

Dedicated to Margaret,

Wife and Partner

65 years

HANS KOESTER TOOK AIR
view of this temple NATIONAL
GEOGRAPHIC
1938

Buddhist temple located at ancient spring in Ordos desert called *Ting Yuan Ning*. The temple is probably one of the most classic pre-revolutionary styles of architecture found anywhere in China. Photo was taken by Rosholt who flew there as a passenger on a Cessna for the Civil Air Transport. Pilot E.V. Wang had to land on a hard, stony field to check his fuel supply before attempting to fly over pass in Heian Mountains, northwest of Ninghsia.

THE STRAYED ARROW

In the village of Grand Spur, there lived a poor couple, who had one daughter named Pearl. This little maid troubled her parents, begging that she might learn to read. They were unable to teach her and none of the neighbors were either. Her parents could not afford to hire a tutor for her and there was no school in the local village. Moreover, it was not customary to instruct girls in the Classics, and girls never associated with boys.

Finally, after much thought they solved their problem by dressing her in boy's clothing, and finding lodging with her maternal grandmother in a neighboring town where she joined the private class of a learned master. There, as a boy, she studied with the boys of her own age, winning praise from her teacher by her diligence and learning, and gaining the admiration of her classmates by her skill in athletic sports, particularly in handling the bow and arrow. She always sat at her desk with a studious and generous boy, named Golden Branch, who was her main companion in work and play, and who became, unknowingly, the possessor of her heart.

The Teacher Expounded a Classic at Eventide Under a Tree. The teacher in this pen drawing sits at center stage, behind a table, probably reading a passage from Mencius or Lao Tze. The pupils are divided into groups according to their age and learning. The older pupils can even bring a fan to class. At lower left, a man with his back towards the groups, is probably a disciplinarian. Times have changed and modern learning in China follows Western procedure and disciplines.

The special troublemaker of the two friends was a rude, sly boy called Grouse, who often interrupted them at their studies, sometimes spoiling their sports events during playtime.

These three, with a dozen other boys, went to the schoolroom before daylight, reading their lessons silently so as to not awaken the teacher who slept in a nearby building.

At dawn the oldest among the pupils knocked at the teacher's door, and invited him to hear their lessons. When the teacher was ready, each pupil came in turn and stood with his back to the teacher, his face to the wall, and recited from memory a quotation from the *Classics of Mencius* and other sages. This morning lesson was twice repeated by the teacher.

Then the boys all went home for breakfast, consisting of boiled rice and salt fish, eaten with chopsticks from a bowl, the chopsticks always held in the right hand.

After breakfast the boys returned to school, swept the room and washed the teacher's dishes and then read out loud, each at his own task. A class in calligraphy or writing with a brush dipped faintly in black ink, they traced the Chinese tze or word in the accepted manner, all beginning at the left side and finishing at the right. Some of the words have as many as ten strokes made with the brush, all traced on a thin, brownish rice paper sheet.

At about noon the teacher assigned each pupil to compose a short poem, and posted the assignment on the back of a door for all to see. This concluded the morning session of school, and the boys ate a noon meal of rice, meats, and chopped vegetables and then worked or played, while thinking about the writing of the poem they were assigned to compose.

It might be an admonition, such as "Go out with awe, come in with fear;" "To a parent be perfectly obedient, to the sovereign be completely loyal," or it might be a proverb, such as

"Tell a stranger only three-tenths of what you know."

On returning to the schoolroom in the middle of the afternoon the boys wrote out the poems they had composed and took them, one by one, to the teacher for comment or correction.

The children then read out loud until sundown when they went to their suppers of rice and vegetables. In the evenings they studied under a lamp, sipping tea and eating cakes.

THE FIVE STRANGE BROTHERS

Once upon a time there was an old woman who had five sons who looked just alike. The oldest could gulp up the ocean at a mouthful; the second was hard enough to nick steel; the third had legs that could be stretched; the fourth was unaffected by fire; the fifth could live without breathing. They all hid their peculiar traits so that the neighbors did not know they were freaks.

The oldest son supported the family by fishing, going alone to the sea, and bringing back a mess of fish. The neighbors begged him to teach their sons how to fish, and finally, one day, he invited them to come along. When he came to shore he sucked the sea into his mouth, and told the boys to step to the bottom to pick up the fish. When he was tired of holding the water, he waved to the boys to return to shore, but they were playing among all the strange objects on the bottom of the sea and paid no attention to him. When he could hold the sea no longer, he had to let it flow back into its former basin and all the boys were drowned. As he walked home he passed the doors of the parents who asked him how many fish their children had caught, and when they would be coming home. He told them what had happened and they became angry and brought him before a judge and accused him of drowning their children. The brother explained how the parents had begged him to take their children fishing. He did not want to but had finally taken them. Then when he urged the children to come from the ocean floor because he couldn't hold the water any longer, and they refused to come, he had to let the water back into the sea basin.

In spite of his defense the judge said that since he had taken the children away and had not returned them he was guilty of murder and the judge sentenced him to be beheaded. But he asked permission before the execution to visit his aged mother, and this was granted. He went alone and told his brothers of his fate, and the second brother returned in his stead to appear before the judge, thanking him for having given him permission to carry out a filial duty and then said he was ready to die. He knelt on his knees, head bowed, and the executioner brought the blade down across the back of his neck, but the sword was only nicked and the head was left intact. A second knife and a third, of finer steel, was brought forward and tried by headsmen who were accustomed to this means of execution. Having spoiled their best blades without a mark on his neck, he was taken back to prison and the judge was informed that the sentence could not be carried out.

The judge then decreed that the defendant should be dropped into the sea and drowned. When the defendant heard this he said that he had told his mother he was leaving her because he had been condemned to execution by beheading, and he now asked permission to return to his mother and explain that he was condemned to be drowned out at sea. The judge agreed he could see his mother a second time and explain the new sentence, by drowning, that awaited him. Having seen his mother he told his brothers what had happened, and the third brother took the place of the second, and presented

himself before the judge as the criminal who was to be drowned at sea. He was then carried from shore and thrown overboard, but he stretched his legs till his feet touched bottom, and there he stood, with his head in the air. He was taken back on board ship and taken farther out to sea and thrown overboard again. But his extendable legs supported him above the water line. Then he was taken into mid-ocean, many miles out, to the South China Sea, but his extendable feet again came to his rescue, and his executioners returned to shore and explained to the judge what had happened and that some other means would have to be found to carry out the sentence.

No one, at first, could think of any new way to carry out the sentence until someone mentioned that the defendant could be boiled in oil, and while the big iron kettle was being heated, the defendant begged for permission to see his mother again to explain that he was going to be boiled in oil.

Now, the brothers, having heard the latest sentence, the fourth brother stepped in and said he would accept the fate of death by being dipped in hot oil. When he was lowered into the burning oil, he acted as though the oil was barely warm and he asked the jailers to stir up the fire to make it hotter. Still, he could not be boiled, and was sent back to prison.

Then everyone in town, the parents, and the judge tried to think of some method of putting him to death. Water, fire, and the sword had all failed. Then they had a new idea, they would

Before the Magistrate. When Go Leng made this pen drawing in the 1870s, the Magistrate was at the peak of his power and authority. In this pen drawing the accused are on their hands and knees, often striking the floor with their heads as a mark of respect and submission to the magistrate who represented the Emperor of China, in the chain of command. His decisions were not to be challenged. At the right are two of the bailiffs, one holding a rawhide or "snake" whip, the other with a long stick of bamboo as an enforcement weapon. Two men at left are probably assistant bailiffs (constables). The magistrate in contemporary China seems to be the hsien-chang, or county chairperson.

smother him in a big cream cake. People all over the country made contributions of flour for the pastry, sugar for the filling and frosting, and bricks for a huge oven. The cake was made and baked on a plain outside the city walls. Meanwhile, the prisoner was allowed to go home to bid his mother farewell and the fifth brother took his place. When the cake was done people pulled it to the execution grounds and the police put the man inside the cake. Since this brother could live without breathing, he rested peacefully until the next evening at which time he safely climbed out of the cake and went home to his brothers and they all lived happily ever after.

THE THREE LUCKY CHARMS

Along the coast of the South Sea, there was a rich man who spent his time and money worshipping the gods. Because he spent so much money helping the poor, he became poor himself, and he had to consider what work he could get to support his wife and three sons. When he found that he could not get a good job near home, he sold all his property, except his house, and went out on a trading expedition to a distant land. On the way he lost all his goods when his junk was wrecked. Now he had to beg for food and clothing, but no one showed him any sympathy. Then one day, a young man gave him a hat, a coat, and a basket, telling him that the hat would make him invisible when he held it in front of his breast, the coat, extended by his arm, would help him to fly over water, and the basket when tapped by his finger, would fill up with precious gems. He took the gifts and found that they did what the man had promised.

The hat allowed him to go places and no one could see him; the coat with arms extended, carried him across the water, and the basket when tapped gave him enough money to buy anything he wanted.

When he reached home he learned that his wife had died while he was gone, and his three sons had grown tall, handsome, and wise. Now the father used his three charms to make them very rich, too. After many years, when he knew he was dying, he called his sons to him and gave them each a charm. To the oldest he gave the coat; to the second the hat; and to his youngest, who was his favorite, he gave the basket. But to each of them he stressed that they should work hard and spend their money wisely.

After the old man had died, the youngest son said he would use his charm to marry a princess. He went to the capital city and found out in which part of the palace the Emperor's daughter lived. Then he looked for the servant girl who took care of the princess and told her that he had precious jewels that he would like to show the princess. The servant gave such a good account of the jewels that the princess sent for them and was so pleased when she saw the jewels she kept them all including the basket. She sent the boy a sum of money which she thought would cover all his expenses. He begged for the return of his basket but the princess refused. Finally, he had to leave without the basket to avoid being arrested for disturbing the peace of the palace.

His means of living having been taken away, he had to beg

The Eight Genii. The word Genii, seldom heard anymore, suggests that this is part of Buddhist mythology, since the number eight carries a special meaning to the followers of the Lord Buddha. Multiples of eight equal sixty-four, and the double of sixty-four is 108, the exact number of beads on a Buddhist rosary.

In the 1920s and 30s, most Chinese dinner parties ended when the waiters brought in the last dish which was called Pa pao fan, or the "eight precious (rice) pudding," a signal, also, that guests could leave.

Using the Wade-Giles system of romanization, Dr. Chester Wang, former head of the Asian collection at Memorial Library, the University of Wisconsin-Madison, has identified the names of the genii in the pen drawing as Han Chung-li, Chang Kuo-lao, T'ien Kuai Li, T'sao Kuo-chiu, Lu Tung-pin, Lan Ts'ai-ho, Han Hsiang-tzu, and Ho Ts'ai-ku (female).

These names, according to Dr. Wang, have been associated as a group since the Yuan, or Mongol Dynasty which ruled China in 1279-1368. It seems extraordinary that the artist, Go Leng, who did this pen drawing in the late 1870s, should include this bit of mythology sponsored by Adele M. Fielde. There are seven male figures in the foreground, which suggests that the female, Ho Ts'ai-ku hovers in space at upper left.

八

for food on the long road home. When he got home he told his brothers what had happened and he wanted to borrow their charms and go back to the palace and get his basket. But his brothers did not want to help him because he had been so careless. Finally they gave in to his nagging and gave him their charms, and he returned to the capital. There he haunted the palace, hoping to find some way to get back his basket. But one day he had his hat on his head instead of in front of his breast, and he was recognized as the man who had caused so much trouble earlier. He was stripped, beaten, and thrown out the gate. Bruised and ashamed to return to his brothers, he wandered off to the deep valleys between the mountains. Hungry, he looked around to see if he could find something to eat. Then he saw two clumps of banana trees with two bunches of fruit, one bunch yellow and ripe, the other bunch green and dried up. At once he ate a ripe banana, but he had no sooner done so than his head began to ache, and on putting up his hand he felt a horn growing from his forehead. The horn grew fast, curled among the trees, and fastened him tightly to the spot. The horror of the situation was extreme, but when he became hungry again, he waited as long as he could but when he could no longer endure starvation, he ate another banana with the same results. He now had a pair of long horns, that he could neither break off nor tear from his head. He again went hungry as long as he could and finally he plucked one of the green bananas. No sooner had he done this than one horn began to shrink, and then disappeared. He then ate another green banana, and the other horn disappeared.

A Blind Fortune-Teller. Pedestrians at right, with youth on step, are asking fortune-teller to pull the right stick from *pi-t'ung* to come up with something that spells "lucky." But two small dogs, resembling terriers, bark at the intrusion. The fortune-teller gets around with cane but it seems he or the dogs have overturned a pot of flowers.

Having returned to normal, he thought to himself that by making use of the fruit that had such qualities he might, perhaps, regain his lost goods. He, therefore, took two of each sort of banana and returned to the palace disguised as a tired traveller. He sent word to the princess that he had come from a fairyland and had a peculiar fruit which would give perpetual youth to whoever ate it. The princess sent her maid to negotiate for the fruit, and the maid, who thought it would be wise for her to remain young with her mistress, bought the two bananas and concealed one in her sleeve while she carried one to the princess. The princess ate the banana and the maid ate hers. As the princess was walking down the stairs, a long horn instantly sprang from her head and coiled among the posts of the divan she was sitting on. A similar horn grew from the head of the maidservant and fastened her to the banister of the stairs. The screams of the two girls aroused all the people in the palace, and, in the confusion, the man with the fruit escaped.

The two girls were in a bad situation. The horns were as sensitive as boils, and as hard as stones. Famous doctors examined them and tried to cut them off. People pleaded with the gods in vain, and the court doctors had all given up hope of removing them. The Emperor then issued a proclamation, promising his daughter in marriage to anyone who could remove the horns from her head. Some time later there came a young man to the palace disguised as a doctor, and presented himself to the Emperor. In the conversation that took place, the Emperor was so impressed by the beauty, good manners, and wisdom of the doctor that he gladly gave his promise that if the doctor removed the horns from the head of the princess and that of her maidservant, the payment would be a legal marriage contract between the princess and the doctor. The doctor then gave each of them a green banana and then had the pleasure of seeing the horns disappear from the head of the bride and her servant. The Emperor kept his word, and the princess went home with her husband carrying the basket, coat, and hat that had been returned to him. When they reached home, the boy returned his brothers' gifts. From that time the family prospered and they all lived happily ever after.

THE ORIGIN OF THE ANTS

Few in our generation of the 1870s remember a man who had a wife who scolded him all the time because he did not make enough money to support their son. She told him that if he could not get enough work around home, he should go somewhere else to work. So he left home looking for work, but he could find nothing and was so homesick that he soon returned home. But he was afraid to go to his own home because he feared his wife would scold him unmercifully. So he sat outside his house, and there he overheard his wife telling their son what she had bought at the market that morning. He heard the cupboard open and close as his wife put away the food. He thought how nice it would be to eat dinner with his family. After a while he got enough courage to go in, but the only greeting he got was, "Why did you come home so soon?"

He replied that while he was gone he had discovered that he had a supernatural sense of smell and he thought he should return and try it out on his friends. His wife laughed at him

Mender of Tubs. In days gone by, China, north to south, was frequented by traveling or mobile menders, ready to fix just about anything on the spot. Most kegs or liquid containers were made of staves which fit together, usually rounded at the middle and tapering off at top and bottom. The mender carries his tools in a box with wheels at the four corners, barely visible. In the box a bow saw is plainly visible. The mender wears grass sandals, suggesting his low rate of pay, while the mistress at right keeps an eye on the vendor. Her hairdo seems unique. Aside from the bow saw, a Western-style ax with short handle is included in the pen drawing by Go Leng (lower left), but this was a tool seldom seen anywhere in China.

and told him to prove it to her. She asked him to tell her what there was to eat in the house. He sniffed the air and said there was an uncooked chicken. His wife was surprised. Then he sniffed again and said there was some pork close to the chicken. He sniffed again and said there was a fish which he thought was carp, in addition to two kinds of vegetables and some bean curd. His wife was so surprised that she gave him his dinner, lovingly. Then she began to brag to her neighbors about the talent her husband had for smelling things, and her story spread far and wide until it reached the ears of the Emperor who was told there was, in a certain village, a man who could find missing things by his sense of smell.

As it happened, the Emperor had lost a jade seal and it was important that it be found. Accordingly, he sent for the wizard and offered him any government office except the throne itself.

The poor man sat down and thought how he could escape punishment for being an impostor. He worried and worried so much that he forgot where he was and started to moan, "This is sharp distress like deep trouble." The people at court, however, thought he had fallen into a trance and would soon tell them where the seal was. Suddenly, he felt his sleeve being pulled and two of the Emperor's men begged him not to betray them for they would show him where the seal was. Thus, he followed the two men, named Sharp and Dyer, who had heard him moan and they thought he was repeating their names. They led him to a well and he told the Emperor that the jade seal was at the bottom. When the bucket was lifted out the Emperor

The Lotus Pool. The ultimate in a leisure society of wealth and splendor seems to be represented in this intricate but provocative pen drawing. The mistress of the house, probably, holds a fan attached to a long, thin handle, which is also carried by another woman, who could be her personal maid. The configuration at left must remain a mystery, for it resembles a tiger's head. The lotus flowers reach the peak of their beauty in August.

offered him the promised award. But the man refused the office. Instead, he chose a coverlet made of candy that his wife could eat at night which would keep her busy and stop her scolding.

The Emperor thought this was a strange request but he had the candy blanket made and the man took it home. His wife was waiting for him, expecting riches and honors, and when he told her he had brought her a blanket of candy she made his life miserable.

Soon after he had left the capital the Empress learned how the Emperor had recovered his seal and she wanted to see for herself, an exhibition of such a wonderful smell. She called the man to her palace, and she wrapped a kitten in raw cotton and put him in a basket. Then she asked the man to tell her what was in the basket. She called all the people in the castle to come and watch this. The poor man did not know what to do. He could not escape because there were so many people around and every door was guarded. He was so afraid of what would happen to him that he exclaimed, "The bagged cat dies!" The Empress, hearing this, hurried to open the basket and discovered that the cat was dead from being wrapped in so much cotton it could not breathe. The people, hearing this, thought that he was a god and his proper place was in heaven, so they tossed him into the heavens. He went so high that when he fell to earth he was nothing but dust. The dust turned into ants and to this day, whenever anyone has anything good to eat, ants find it by their keen sense of smell.

THE MISTAKE OF THE APES

Not far from Swatow, there was a lazy man who had a wife who also scolded him all the time. He got so tired of her nasty tongue that he went into the woods to hang himself. As he tied the noose around his neck his courage failed, and he went back home. When his wife saw him she said that he had been gone so long that she was hoping he would never come back. This wounded his feelings so much that he told his wife he was going to the woods to hang himself. She did not try to stop him.

In the forest he walked from tree to tree but could not find one that satisfied him. He walked some more and finally came to a strange place. He sat down, but was so tired and hungry he fell into a deep sleep. Presently, he was discovered by a wandering ape who reported to his tribe that he had found their ancestor. A council of elders was called around the sleeping man, and after looking him over very carefully, they decided that he was their ancestor and should be their king and they carried him to their place in a wooded valley and put him on a throne. When he woke up he was surrounded by apes who gave him anything he could eat and drink and he enjoyed being king of the apes. They continued to bring him valuable gifts from near and far. They also showed him where they kept all the valuable articles they had accumulated over the years.

One day, when the apes were away, he took all their wealth

that he could carry, made his way out of the forest and returned to his home. His wife, who thought he was just as shabby as before, started to scold him but he stopped her by putting a gold piece in her hand. She realized there was enough to live on for many years, and she became more friendly. She soon told her close friends that her husband had gone out to hang himself, and had come home rich. One of her friends told her husband about this and told him to do likewise. Then the man asked his neighbor to tell him how he had acquired all his wealth. The man said he would never tell anyone and, besides, he would give him half his wealth when he got it. So the man told his neighbor how to get to the place under the trees where he had been seated, and the man followed his directions and waited for the apes to come and get him.

The apes, meanwhile, decided that the being who had stolen all their wealth was neither related to them nor was he their king. When one of the apes was looking around for things to collect, he saw the second man under the tree, and reported this back to his tribe. This made the apes very angry. They surrounded him and tore him to pieces.

A Beggar and His Blind Wife. The beggar holds the staff which his wife clings to, while at the same time he holds up a bowl for the man at the window, probably a merchant, who is already donating a coin. The person at the corner at upper right looks on, seemingly, without pity. In all the pen drawings which Adele M. Fielde asked Go Leng to do, no suggestion is ever made to foot binding, which began in the Sung Dynasty, a custom observed by women in all walks of life, rich or poor.

八

八

THE MOON CAKE

Once there was a little boy who had a cake that a big boy wanted. The latter wanted to get the cake without making the little boy cry or call for his mother. The older boy thought that the cake would be prettier if it looked like the moon and the little boy agreed. The big boy said he had made many moons, and the little boy gave him his cake. The big boy took a big bite, leaving the crescent with jagged edges. At this point the little boy became unhappy with the results and started to cry. The big boy stopped him by saying he could make the cake into a half moon. So he nibbled off the edges of the crescent to make it look like a half moon. Seeing this the little boy started to cry since there was hardly any cake left. Then the big boy said he would make it into a full moon. But, remember this, he said, that before the rise of the new moon the old one disappears. Then he swallowed the rest of the cake and left the little boy waiting for the new moon.

Consulting a Soothsayer. Here a customer, hands in his sleeves but at the back, wants to have his fortune told. All he has to do is put down his money and the fortune-teller will pull a stick out of the receptacle. The customer apparently has his choice of sticks. The scroll at the back could be a poster of self-advertising. The elderly man at right holds his hands in his sleeves but in right hand probably holds a fan, the earmark of gentility.

A FOOL WHO TRIED TO BE LIKE HIS BROTHER-IN-LAW

In the 1870s people remembered the rich widow who had an only son, who was a fool. She had gotten him a pretty young wife from a rich family. When the time came for the bridegroom to pay his first visit to his bride's family, his mother was anxious that he should not disgrace her by bad manners, so she gave him special instructions on how to behave himself while a guest in his father-in-law's house.

Knowing that the older sister of the bride was married to a man of good reputation and was considered bright, the mother could think of no better way for her son to act but to follow everything the man did and that he should do likewise.

When the son returned home after his visit to his father-in-law's house, his mother asked if he had done everything his brother-in-law had done. Her son answered: "I did everything that Mr. Blank did in all things but one; I failed to froth at the mouth." The man she had appointed as a pattern for her son had thrown a fit and the son had thrown himself on the floor like his brother-in-law but he could not froth at the mouth. From this comes the common saying: "Don't try to be just like your brother-in-law."

A DREADFUL BOAR

One of Ms. Adele Fielde's storytellers described a poor old woman who lived with her one little granddaughter. One day she was out gathering wood for the stove when she found a stalk of sugar cane which she added to the bundle. Presently, she met a fairy in the form of a wild boar who asked her for the sugar cane but she said that it was hard for her to bend down and when she picked something up she kept it for herself and her little granddaughter. The boar got very angry at her for her refusal and told her that he would come that night and eat her granddaughter instead of the cane, and disappeared into the woods.

When the old woman got home, she sat down by the door of her cabin and cried aloud because she knew she had no way of protecting herself against the boar. While she sat crying a peddler came by selling needles and asked her what was the matter. She told him about the boar and he said that all he could do for her was to give her some needles. This he did and went on his way. The old woman stuck needles thickly over the lower half of her door on the outside, and then she went on crying.

Just then a man came along with a basket of crabs and heard her crying and stopped to ask her what was wrong with her. When she told him, he said he did not know what to do for her but he would give her half of his crabs. The old woman put the crabs in a water jar and again sat down and cried.

After a while a farmer came by leading his ox. When she told him her sad story, he said he could think of nothing he could do for her but he would leave his ox with her overnight to keep her from getting lonesome. She took the ox into the house and tied it to the head of her bed and gave it some straw, and then began to cry again. A messenger returning on horseback from a neighboring town stopped to ask what her trouble was. When she told him he said he would leave his horse with her to make the ox more content. So she tied the horse to the foot of her bed, but then she cried more because it was getting late and she did not know how to prevent the evil that was coming.

Just then a boy came along with a snapping turtle. When she told him her troubles, he said there was no way to stop fairies but he would give her his snapping turtle to show his sympathy. She took the turtle, tied it to the foot of her bed and started to cry again.

Some men carrying millstones came by and asked her what her trouble was. When she told them, they said they did not know how to help her but they could give her a millstone which they left in her backyard. A little later a man arrived carrying hoes and pickaxes, and when she told him her troubles, he said he could do nothing for her because he was only a well digger, but he could dig a well for her. She pointed out a place in the backyard and he went to work and dug her a well. The old woman began crying again, until a paper seller came along and asked her what was the matter. When she told him he gave her a large sheet of paper which he put over the well to show his sympathy.

A Barber Shaving the Head. A mobile or transient barber will shave or cut hair anywhere. He brings his own hot water heater, and in this scene the customer seems to be collecting what the barber cuts or shaves off. The barber wears a queue, but the customer must be someone special, for his headgear seems uncommon.

Nightfall came; the old woman shut and barred the door, put her granddaughter on the wall side of the bed, and then lay down to wait.

At midnight a boar came and threw himself against the door to break in. The needles hurt him badly, and by the time he broke in, he was overheated and thirsty and went to the water jar to drink. When he pushed in his snout, crabs attacked him, clung to his bristles and pinched his ears till he rolled over and over to get rid of them. Then, in a rage, he approached the front of the bed but the snapping turtle nipped his tail, and forced him to retreat under the feet of the horse, who kicked him over to the ox, while the ox tossed him back to the horse. By this time he was glad to escape to the backyard and rest, wondering what to do next. Seeing a clean piece of paper spread over the ground, he went to lie upon it, and fell into the well. The old woman heard the fall, rushed out, and rolled the millstone down the well and that was the end of the dreadful boar!

Ploughing. The Chinese plow, according to legend, was invented by an emperor named Shen Nung, god of agriculture. Since Chinese civilization developed about the same time as the Egyptians and Persians, which is to say several thousand years B.C., it seems fair to assume that the Chinese claim can be considered valid. The land under cultivation lay along the Yellow River, most likely, and people moved from a hunting society to a domestic society of permanent settlement and planted grains from nature that could be replanted from season to season. The plow shown here in Go Leng's pen drawing shows a shallow plowshare.

八

THE YOUNG HEAD OF THE FAMILY

There was this family, the father, his three sons, and two daughters-in-law, wives of the two elder sons who had recently been brought into the house, and were both from a village a few miles away. Having no mother-in-law living they had to appeal to the father-in-law whenever they wanted to visit their former homes, and, as they were homesick, they were perpetually begging the old man to go home.

Irritated by these constant petitions, he worked out a method to put an end to their carping. "You are always asking me to allow you to go home to visit your mothers, and I know you think I am hard-hearted if I do not let you go, but now you may go, but only upon one condition: when you come back you will each bring me something I need. One of you will bring me some fire wrapped in a paper, and the other some wind in a paper, and if you fail to get these for me, you are never to return.

The old man did not think that these conditions would be accepted, but the girls were young and thoughtless, and in their anxiety to get away did not consider the impossibility of getting the articles required. So they hurried home. After they had walked a long distance, talking about who they should see and what they would do in their native village, the high heel of one of the girls slipped from under her foot, and she fell. Both stopped to adjust the shoe, and while doing so, they thought of the conditions under which they could return to their husbands and both began to cry.

At this point a young girl came riding from the paddy fields on a water-buffalo. She stopped and asked them what they were crying about and if she could help them. They said she could not help them. But she persisted in offering her sympathy and asking how she could help them. Finally, they told her their story. At once, she said that if they went home with her she would show them a way out of their troubles. The case seemed so hopeless to them, but the girl was so sure she could help them, that they finally went with her to her father's house where she showed them how to get what their father-in-law had demanded.

To begin with, they would need a paper lantern. When lighted, it would be a fire, and the paper surrounding it would go around the blaze, so it would truly be "some fire wrapped in paper." For the second a paper fan would suffice. When the fan was waved wind would blow from it and "wind wrapped in paper" could be carried to the old man.

The two young girls thanked the wise child, and went on their way happy as larks. After a pleasant visit to their old homes, they took a lantern and a fan, and returned to their father-in-law's house. As soon as he saw them, he began to show his anger at their light regard for his commands. But they assured him that they had obeyed him perfectly. Then they showed him what they had brought fulfilled the conditions he had made. Much surprised he asked them how they had suddenly become so smart, and they told him of their journey and of the little girl who had come to their aid. He asked them if the little girl was already betrothed, and learning that she was not, he hired a go-between to see if he could get her as a wife for his youngest son.

Having succeeded in getting the girl as a daughter-in-law, he brought her home, and told all the rest of the family that, as there was no mother in the family, and as the young girl had shown that she was very wise, she would be made the head of the household.

A big wedding was held and the sons of the old man were to return to their usual occupations on the farm; but according to their father's order, they now had to go to the young bride for instructions. She told them that they were never to go to or from fields empty-handed. When they went to work, they must carry fertilizers of some sort for the land, and when they returned they must collect bundles of sticks for fuel. They obeyed, and soon the land was in good condition and so much fuel had been gathered that there was no need to buy any. When there were no more sticks, roots, or weeds to bring, she told them to bring stones instead. They soon accumulated an immense pile of stones, which were heaped near the house.

One day an expert in precious stones came along, and saw in the pile of stones, a piece of jade of great value. In order to get the jade at a low price, he said he wanted to buy the whole heap of stones. The young head of the family asked an exorbitant price for them. He could not get her to cut down the price so he said he would pay her the sum she asked. Then he said he would come back two days later to bring her the money. After he had gone, the young girl thought about the reason for the buyer's willingness to pay so much for the stones, and

A Young Girl Came from the Fields, Riding on a Water Buffalo. This was a common scene in the Chinese countryside even after World War II. The buffalo was controlled through a ring in its nose. The farmers seemed to take pride in the sharply-pointed horns, suggesting a strong male, but these pointed horns were dangerous, and one of the main reasons for personal injury at hospitals and clinics.

decided that the heap must contain a rare gem. The next morning she sent her father-in-law to invite the buyer for supper and told the men of the family about entertaining him. They were to provide the best of wines, and the father-in-law was to get him to talk about precious stones, and ask him how to identify the different stones.

The young head of the family, listening behind a curtain heard how the valuable stone in the heap could be discovered. She hurried out to find it and remove it from the pile. When the guest had recovered from the effects of the banquet he found that the price was much higher than they had decided on at first. He went to negotiate again with the seller, and she conducted the conference with such skill that she got the price that they had originally agreed upon for the heap of stones and a large sum for the stone in her possession.

The family, having become wealthy, built an ancestral hall of fine design and elaborate workmanship, and etched the words: "NO SORROW," as an inscription over the entrance gate.

Soon after, a Mandarin official passed this way, and noticing this remarkable inscription, he ordered his sedan-chair set down, so that he could ask who the people were who said they had no sorrow. He sent for the head of the family, and was surprised to see so young a woman. He said, "Yours is a remarkable family. I have never before heard of a family without sorrow, nor one with so young a person at the head. I will fine

A Mandarin in His Sedan-Chair. Before the advent of the railroad and the 40-seat bus came to China, travel from town to town, or village to canal, was usually by sampans or small boats, and junks, but most people walked or drove astride an ass or mule. But a girl en route to her future husband's house or compound would, if she was among the elite, arrive in a sedan chair as shown here, and of course, the "mandarin" here is no common stick along the river; he is most likely a high official, or hsien-chang (a magistrate) who was entitled to all the perks that came with high office.

you for your impudence. Go weave me a piece of cloth as long as the road," ordered the Mandarin.

"Very well," said the head of the family; "as soon as your Excellency has found the two ends of the road, and informed me as to the number of feet in its length, I will begin weaving at once."

The Mandarin realized he had made a mistake, but he added, "And I also fine you as much oil as there is in the sea."

"Certainly," she said, "as soon as you measure the sea, and send me correct information as to the number of gallons of water there are in the sea, I will begin to press out the oil from my beans."

"Indeed!" said the Mandarin. "Since you are so smart, perhaps you can penetrate my thoughts. If you can, I will fine you no more. I hold this pet bird in my hand, now tell me whether I mean to squeeze it to death or let it fly into the air?"

"Well," said the youthful head of the family, "I come from an obscure family and you are a famed magistrate. If you do not have any more brains than I, you have no right to fine me at all. Now, I stand with one foot on one side of the door, and the other foot on the other side; tell me whether I mean to go in or to come out. If you cannot guess my riddle, you should not require me to guess yours."

Unable to guess her intentions, the Mandarin left, and the family continued to prosper, living happily under the young leader.

THE SPOON THAT FELL FROM THE MOON

It's hard to imagine, but in a distant town there was an old woman who lived by cheating her relatives and neighbors. Her husband lived alone with his only son in a house nearby. One day the son brought home his bride, and the old woman went to call on her. She asked the young bride if she had heard any scratching among the boxes containing her wedding outfit. The bride said no, she had not. A few days later the old woman came to visit again, and then the young bride said she had been listening and she had heard some scratching among her boxes. The woman advised her to examine her clothes carefully, because, evidently, there were mice in the house and they might at any time find her clothes and nibble them to shreds. The old lady knew there was no cat in the house, nevertheless, she asked the bride if they had one and hearing that they did not, she offered to lend the young woman her own black and white cat. She said that the cat would soon kill all the mice. The bride accepted the loan, and the old woman brought the cat and left it in the bride's apartment. After a few hours the cat disappeared. The bride, thinking it had gone home, did not look for it. The cat had indeed gone home, and the old woman killed the cat and buried it without anyone seeing what she had done.

A few days later she came back and said that when she had lent her the cat there were no mice in her house, but as soon as the cat left, the mice came back and multiplied so fast that now her house was overrun by them and that she would have to ask for the return of her cat. The young woman said that the cat had left the same day that it came and she figured it had gone home. The old woman said that it had not, and that nothing could compensate her for the loss of the cat which she herself had raised from a tiny kitten, and that there had never been such a cat for catching mice. A cat, spotted as that one, was seldom found, and that it was such a rare breed that had given rise to the common saying:

"A coal-black mouser, with white loins
Is worth its weight in silver coins."

The young woman was very surprised by this estimate of the cat's value, and she went to her father-in-law and told him what had happened. The father-in-law knowing the character of the old woman, was afraid she would worry his daughter-in-law until the two hundred ounces of silver was paid. But the young woman, being a newcomer, did not know what the woman was like so she did not worry about it until the woman had come many times to talk about the cat. When the young

Peasant Girl and Student. The student in this pen drawing is at lower left, holding a round fan, probably of bamboo and leaves of the bamboo tree, a clear signal that he is not a person who has to work for a living like the peasant girl at upper right who is using the pole *(pien-tan)*, which G.I.s in World War II called "yo-yo" poles. U.S. air bases and the Burma road were built largely by Chinese workers, men and women, using this pole to carry earth and crushed rock to the road or runways. The peasant girl is bringing two bunches of brush and grass to heat up the small stoves in the kitchen, not to heat the room but to boil hot water for tea or to warm up a bowl of wine. Tea bushes were grown in Chekiang and Fukien provinces, but the tea which passengers on trains sipped was from green tea leaves, which are grown on hillsides that can not be cultivated for rice. But those who could afford the best had black tea imported from Ceylon (now as Sri Lanka).

woman realized she would have to defend herself, she went to her father-in-law and asked if he had ever lent anything to the woman. He could think of nothing, but she told him to think carefully and finally he said he had once lent her a wooden spoon which had cost only a few dollars and was not worth speaking about.

The next time that the old woman came to ask for the money to pay for her cat, the young woman asked her to return the wooden spoon she had borrowed. The old woman said the spoon was worthless; she had let the kids play with it in the dirt and there it had lain until she picked it up and used it as wood for the stove. The bride replied: "You want to enrich yourself and your family by your cat. I and my family also want money. Since you can not give back the spoon we will go to the magistrate and present our cases. If your cat is judged to be worth more than my spoon, then I will pay what is left over, but if my spoon is judged to be worth more than your cat, you will pay me." The old woman, thinking that any judge would consider her cat worth more than a wooden spoon, she agreed to go the the magistrate. The young woman very politely let the old woman go first to make the accusation. She told about the loss of her cat and that the cat was worth two hundred ounces of silver. Then the judge called on the young woman for her defense. She said she would not deny that the cat had been lost, but that the old lady had borrowed a wooden spoon and had never returned it to her father-in-law. There is common saying:

Father and Father-In-Law. Even before puberty, children of the elite, merchant or shipbuilder were predestined to find a mate because their parents had already arranged to a match. As seen here the father of either a boy or girl meets his prospective counterpart; all with the greatest ceremony and formality, both sides angling for some advantage over the other. Note the intricate woodwork of chairs and the table. A vase of fresh flowers always in place. But the beards on the two elders seem exaggerated.

"In the moon overhead, at its full, you can see
The trunk, branches, and leaves of a cinnamon tree."

A branch from this tree had one night been blown down before her father-in-law's door and he had a spoon made from the wood. Whenever the spoon was dipped into anything (syrup, wine, etc.) it never got less with use. A foreign innkeeper hearing of this magic spoon had offered her father-in-law three thousand ounces of gold for it, but the offer was refused. This wooden spoon was the one that the old lady had borrowed and destroyed.

Then the judge realized that the cat had been used as a means of extortion, and he judged that the two claims offset each other so that no payment was due from anyone.

THE STOLEN GARLIC

A poor man planted a bed of garlic. Because he had no land besides the plot, he tended each plant separately and the plants grew fast. When the crop was almost large enough to pull, he put a little cabin beside the little bed of garlic and slept there to guard the garlic from thieves. After watching for many nights he decided there were no thieves around and he went home to sleep in his own bed. But he left the little cabin there. When he came back the next day to water his vegetables he saw that they had all been pulled and carried away.

In distress and grief he went to the magistrate and complained of his loss. The magistrate asked him why he did not seize the thief.

"Because, your honor, I was not there when he came."

"Then, why did you not bring some garlic from the garden so that it might be traced?"

"Because he left nothing but the movable cabin that was there before."

"Very well," said the magistrate; "Since the cabin was the only object in the field at the time of the theft, we will make the cabin the defendant in the suit, and you will appear tomorrow morning here as the plaintiff against it."

When word got around about the complaint and that a movable cabin would be charged with theft, the people poured into the courtroom. The police brought in the movable cabin and put it in the place for prisoners. It was charged with the crime but could not offer any defense. The magistrate ordered that the cabin should be beaten until it confessed. The police administered the blows until the cabin fell to pieces. The audience watched, and then they began to laugh and they laughed and laughed because it was such a good joke.

The magistrate became very angry and he charged the whole court with contempt, ordered all doors locked, and fined each person a pound of garlic and no release until the fine was paid. The police went with the people so they could buy a pound of garlic to pay their fines and each was happy to pay the small amount of money it took to buy the garlic.

During the course of the day, all the garlic in the market had been bought and all the garlic in the neighboring towns had been bought.

As each person handed in his fine, he was required to tell where he got the garlic. When all the garlic had been collected, the plaintiff was asked to examine the bunches of garlic and to tell whether any of it looked like his own. He looked and said that certain bunches were his. Then the police looked up where the garlic had been bought and all the bunches were found to have been bought from one green-grocer.

The green-grocer was arrested and forced to tell who he had bought it from. He named a certain man in the village. The man was arrested and was proven by circumstantial

The Bridge. While this arched bridge was modeled after a bridge on a river near Shandou, the same type of bridge may be found all over south China. Old beliefs, mostly superstition, held that no bridge need be higher than a man could walk under along the bank. Sanpans approaching these bridges had to lower all sails to get under, a matter that caused delay and often outright fighting. In this drawing Go Leng has three men in a boat or sanpan negotiating the passage. These bridges were built of stone-marble, with fancy posts, essentially a public donation by someone who wished to display not his community spirit but his self-esteem.

evidence to have been the thief. The magistrate got a great reputation for wisdom, the thief got forty blows, and the poor gardener got all the garlic that had been collected as fines for contempt of court.

TWO STINGY MEN

A stingy man who was going on a journey took with him rice to boil for his meals and a salt shrimp spice to mix when his rice seemed tasteless. As he was eating his plain food, he noticed another traveler put his chopsticks into a little jar and put them empty into his mouth. He wondered how there could be any one who seemed more careful with his money than he, so he walked over to the man and asked him to explain what he was doing, putting his chopsticks into a jar and coming out empty. The man said that he had some brine in the bottle, and he dipped his chopsticks in that when he wanted to add some taste to his food. So the two men who seemed to have similar habits became good friends.

It seemed that the man who tasted the brine had a marriageable son, while the man who sold salt shrimp had a daughter of the same age. The two became engaged to be married and that made the two men related.

On a trip the brine taster found that he would have to pass the home of the shrimp man. That gave him a chance to visit his relative. He was received with great demonstrations of pleasure, and the guest heard the host give the order to his wife to go and buy a big fish at least six inches long and cook it for their supper. When his wife returned with the fish the host thought the fish was too large for one meal, so he told his wife to cut it in half and put one half in vinegar to pickle and the other half, the one with the tail should be fried. When the guest sat down to eat and saw the fish, he said that his host should not have been so extravagant, and then rather then put his host to the added expense of giving him breakfast, he would leave before breakfast. The next morning he left with many expressions of regret that he had caused his friend so much expense.

When he reached home he found that he had a guest who had arrived just before he did. His wife suggested that he go to the store and buy something to eat. The man took his basket and started for the store. On the way he was thinking of what he had had the night before and he sent a messenger to his friend and said that he had company when he got home. He asked him if he might borrow the pickled fish for his company. When the messenger returned, he brought the fish and a letter saying: "Since it is you who asks for the fish, I must send it. But do not put it in water to soften it but fry it hard so that the chopsticks will not go into the fish and then you can send it back to me intact."

A Man Returning From Abroad. A young man wearing long braid or queue is presenting a gift to the elderly lady, perhaps his grandmother, who walks with the help of a long cane with knot at the top to suggest longevity, if not class privilege. A servant with *pien-tan* or carrying pole, follows the traveler with gifts and boxes, while a second servant carries a chest on his shoulders, a symbol of an important merchant. The girl at lower right carries bamboo fan and wears a string of beads, perhaps a Buddhist rosary. Going abroad in the 1870s usually meant a visit to Singapore, or the Philippines, or even Thailand, but not Japan which was recouping from the Meiji Restoration of 1868.

THE MOST MISERLY OF MEN

At one time people pointed to a man in Swatow who was the most miserly man in the city. But others heard there was a man who was actually the most miserly in all of China. The Swatow man said to his son, "We live on very little, but if we were more frugal we might live on nothing. It will be worth our while to visit this man and learn how he manages to stay alive. The son agreed, and the two decided that the son should go. But there would have to be an exchange of gifts. The father told his son to take a penny and buy a piece of paper. By bargaining he got two sheets of the cheapest paper. The father put away one sheet and cut the other in half, and on one half he drew a picture of a pig's head. This he put into a basket as if it were the thing it represented. A pig's head was the usual gift sent as a show of great respect. The son took the basket and after a long journey reached the home of the most miserly man in all of China.

The master of the house was gone, but his son met and received the traveler, learned his errand, and accepted the offering. He took the picture of the pig's head and said courteously to his visitor, "I am sorry we have nothing in the house that is worthy of the pig's head in your basket. I will, however, show our friendly reception of it by putting four oranges in the basket for you to take home with you."

Then the young man, without having any oranges to give him, made the motions with his hand that were necessary to put the oranges into the basket. Then the son returned and told his father about thrift that was greater than theirs.

When the most miserly man in all of China returned home, his son told him that a visitor from a long way off had come to learn about economy from him. The father asked what offering he had brought as an introduction and the son showed the small picture of a pig's head on a half sheet of brown paper. Then the father asked his son what he had sent in return and the son showed how he had made the motions with his hand to put oranges in the visitor's basket. The father flew into a rage. "You extravagant wretch. With your fingers spread so far apart you appeared to give him big oranges. Why didn't you measure out small ones?"

THE TWO MELONS

There was a time when a poor but honest woman was washing clothes at a local pool. While there a bird fell down that a hunter had disabled in one wing, by an arrow. The woman gently picked up the bird, carried it home, dressed its wounds, and fed it until the wing was healed. It then fled into the air and away.

A few days later the bird returned and recognized the leaf of a melon. The woman made a trellis for it and it grew to a large size. Next, the woman was surprised a short time later when the bird returned and laid an oval seed in front of her and then disappeared. The woman planted the seed in her garden and when it came up she recognized the leaf of a melon. Toward the end of the year the old woman was unable to pay her debts, and her poverty made her so unhappy that she became sick. Sitting at the door one day, she saw that the melon was ripe and it looked delicious. She decided to try it and see if it was as good as it looked. Taking a knife, she cut through the melon, and was surprised to hear that it rattled in her hands, and when she cut into it again it was filled with

Women at a Shrine. Women, wearing various hairstyles, are on their knees at a shrine, probably Buddhist, to light incense sticks seen on the table flanked by candleholders. A curtain has been lifted at the back to reveal a statue seated on lotus leaves. The worshippers have also brought food which was carried by servant at right. All the women wear flowers in their hair. The statue could be Kuanyin, the goddess of mercy.

gold and silver coins. She used these coins to pay all her debts and bought enough supplies for many days.

Among the old woman's neighbors was a busybody who found out how the old lady had suddenly become so rich. Thinking that there was no reason why she too should not be equally lucky, she went to the same pool to wash clothes until she managed to hurt one of the birds flying over the water. She took the wounded bird home and treated it with care until the wing was healed, and the bird flew away. Shortly after it returned with a seed in its beak, laid it before her and then flew away. The woman quickly planted the seed, saw it come up and spread its leaves, and made a trellis for it. She became very happy when she saw the melon spread its vines and saw a melon growing. While waiting for her future wealth, she ate too much rich food, and bought fine clothes and before the end of the year went deeply into debt. But the melon was growing day by day, and she was delighted to see it ripen into large size, and then she too heard a rattling inside of the melon.

At the end of the year she cut the vine down and cut the melon open, expecting it to be full of coins; but in it there were two lame and hungry beggars who said they would remain to live with her the rest of their lives!

An Apothecary's Shop. The shop or store front usually opens directly on the street curb. It has no front windows or doors. At night it is boarded up completely from one end to the other to discourage theft. The customers at the right wear queue, or "pigtails." A woman, no doubt part of the family who operated this store, seems to be drumming up business, probably offering a better deal than her competitors across the street. The bottles all have lids. What kind of drugs are they selling? Herbs or ground up rhinoceros horns imported from India or Africa. The majority of the customers were men who drank these powders in their tea in the belief that it gave them more strength sexually.

THE FAIRY SERPENT

In a village on the Han River which flows into Shandao Harbor there was a man who had three daughters whom he loved very much. They were skilled in embroidery, and every day on his way home from work he picked up some flowers that they could use as patterns. But one day he could find no flowers on his way home, so he went in the woods to look for some. But in doing so, he unknowingly invaded the home of the fairy serpent who became quite angry and scolded the man for butting in. The man excused himself and said he was looking for a few flowers to bring home to his daughters who would naturally be disappointed if he came home empty-handed. The snake asked the names, the numbers, and the ages of his daughters and then refused to let him go unless he promised one of them in marriage to him. The poor man used every argument he could think of to make the snake let him go but he would not. The father agreed to the proposition and returned home. He could eat no supper because he knew the power of the fairies and he was afraid of what would happen to the whole family if he did not fulfill his promise.

Some days passed, his girls made him special food for his

A Flower Show. The competition to grow the most gorgeous flowers comes to a head with an annual show and oversized porcelain vases. Most of the onlookers here are men but the suggestion of a gray-beard (center right) seems unreal. The youth in lower right views the display in classic stance, hands in his sleeves, at his back.

八

meals but he could not eat. He sat in sorrowful meditation. His daughters talked among themselves about what could be causing him so much sorrow. Then they decided that each one in turn would talk to their father and find out why he would not eat. The eldest daughter went first and expressed her concern at his not eating. Finally he told her that he would eat if she, for his sake, would marry the snake to whom he had promised a wife.

She bluntly refused to carry out the promise. Then the second daughter went to talk to him and he asked her the same question and she also refused. The the youngest daughter went to see him and asked him to eat. He gave her the same answer, if she would wed the snake, he would eat. When she heard his story she said if he would take good care of his health, she would wed the serpent. So he ate again and everything returned to normal in their home.

But one morning as the girls were sewing, a wasp flew into the room and sang:

"Buzz! I buzz buzz and come the faster;
Who will wed the snake my master?"

Whenever the wasp alighted the girls stuck him with their needles and followed him up so closely that he had to flee for

The Musicians. The Chinese orchestra, in a sense, which provided musical accompaniment for opera and drama for actors such as Mei Lan-fang, in the 1920s and 1930s. Here, the musicians include two-stringed Chinese violins. At the right the player holds a p'i-pa (pronounced pee-bah) which has four strings. There is also a stringed instrument which resembles a viola. The long pipe-like instrument the player is holding can be called a flute. In top center one of the musicians is using a percussion instrument, probably as a conductor's baton, one rumble often bringing the house down. The utensils in the foreground include small cups for either tea or wine, the earthen object could be shielding a flame to keep the tea or wine warm. An effort is being made by a musicians' group in Shanghai to continue the ancient music, but the signs point in the other direction, since modern Chinese opera fans love Bach and Grieg and have fingerpickers from around the world appearing in concert.

his life. The next day two wasps came and sang the same song, and the girls stuck them with needles and they had to flee. The third day, three wasps came, and each day the wasps increased in number until the girls could not stand the stings.

Then the youngest daughter said, that in order to stop the buzzing plague, she would go to the bridegroom. The wasps accompanied her on the road and took her to the place where the fairy serpent was waiting for her in a large palace he had built for her. There were large rooms with carved furniture, inlaid with precious stones, chests full of silk clothes, and caskets full of jade and jewels of gold. The snake had beautiful eyes and a musical voice; but his skin was warty and the girl shuddered at having to see him every day.

After the wedding supper, which the two shared alone, she told him she appreciated the beautiful home he had provided for her and that she would do all the housework and take care of him. She did all the housework and was so kind to him that he could not stand it when she had to go on errands. She began to enjoy him too, so much that she forgot how repulsive he looked.

She did not have any help with her housework, so one day when the well dried up, she had to go into the woods, looking for water. She found the water, but then had to carry it home in a large pail. When she came home she found the snake was dying of thirst, so she plunged him into the water and he arose from the water transformed into a strong and handsome man. He had been changed into a snake by a wicked fairy and her kindness and care of him broke the spell and set him free. After that she and her husband visited her home and carried gifts to those who were less happy than she.

WHAT THE BIRDS SAID

There was a boy named Chiang who lived with his parents in the mountains. Chiang could understand the language of birds. One evening as he sat reading, a flock of birds roosted in a tree in front of his window and began to sing:

"Chiang, on the southern plain
A sheep waits for you by a heap of stones -
A fine, fat sheep, that the dogs have killed;
You eat the flesh and we will pick the bones!"

Chiang went and picked up the sheep and brought it home and cooked it that evening. The next morning a shepherd came by and said one of his sheep was missing, and that he had found blood in the meadow, and that he had followed the trail and it had brought him to this house. Chiang admitted that he had taken in the sheep but he declared that the dogs had killed it. Its death and place where he could find it had been told to him by the birds. The shepherd did not believe him and Chiang was hauled before a judge who sent him to prison. While he was waiting for his trial, a bird flying by, saw him and sang:

"Foes approach the western border,
Banners, bows, and spears in order,
While the gate lacks watch or policeman."

Chiang told the jailer to inform the magistrate of the danger that was approaching the unprotected Western Pass. The jailer did not believe him but decided to test him to see if he really could understand what the birds were singing. He took some rice and soaked it in sweetened water and some in vinegar and spread it over the roof of a shed that he brought Chiang to, and asked him if he knew why so many birds were chirping overhead. Chiang replied that those on the roof were calling to those who were flying by and singing:

"Call a halt, call a halt;
Here is rice fresh and white
Half is sweet and half is salt;
Stop a bit; take a bite."

The jailer was now convinced that Chiang could understand the speech of birds, so he hurried to the magistrate and reported the warning and the test. The magistrate sent a swift messenger to warn the military officers, and a scout was sent out to the west. The scout confirmed Chiang's warning and troops were sent to the pass to strengthen it. The invaders were successfully defeated and Chiang was considered a hero. The king made use of his great talent, invited him to study with the prince, and finally raised him to a high rank among the nobles.

Archery Practice. A young man, riding a horse, turns in the saddle to shoot an arrow into a portable target (at left). Portable target has carved claws for legs, and the bull's-eye can be seen in center of target. The archer rides his horse with only a halter, but horse is trained to run or turn by pressure of knees of rider in front of stirrup. The rider wears riding boots, as do the three other contestants. A fourth figure, also wearing boots, is in charge of kettle drum which, probably, is struck if rider scores a bull's-eye. Horse is not a Mongol or an Arab, but artist Go Leng has caught the outstretched legs of horse, front and back, and the speed can be measured by the outstretched tail.

THE MAN IN THE SHELL

At another time there was a woman who was so anxious to have a grandson that she visited all the shrines in her neighborhood to make offerings and pray that her only son's wife would have a child. When she had prayed in vain to all the gods in her neighborhood and still had no grandson, she began to think of the Sea Dragon King. Although she had never heard of anyone praying to the Dragon asking for a child she decided to do anything she could think of. So she prayed and prayed to the Dragon King. A water snake sent word to the Dragon King that there was a woman worshipping him on the beach, and he sent a fish to find out what she wanted. The fish, having heard her prayers, brought back a report that she wanted a grandson. The Sea Dragon laughed and said, "We have no humans here. If she wants a grandson from me she will have to take a shell. That is the best I can give her."

Time passed, and the old woman had expectation of the fulfillment of her wishes. The Sea Dragon's meritorious agency

Worshipping at the Grave of an Ancestor. Here members of a family assemble, probably at the Spring Festival not to "sweep the tombs," but to make offerings to the spirits of the deceased. A fish resembling a big perch lies on a tray, and at left in bowl may be *man-tou,* or steamed bread buns, and in another platter are fruits. Behind these edibles are bowls heaped with rice and chopsticks to eat with. The two objects that flank the food stuffs may be lanterns. There is no name on the headstone but everyone knows who is buried here. After bowing several times to the spirits of the departed, the family takes the food home and eats it, or the eating may start at the graveside. The men at upper right all hold their hands in their sleeves.

was acknowledged, praised, and rumored abroad. The child was in due time born, and was found to be encased in a spiral shell, with his head projecting from its mouth. As the family was a wealthy one, the strange babe was skillfully cared for. When he grew older, he would come out of his shell, as does a snail, but would withdraw quickly into it again when tired or frightened. After he attained the size of a man, he would frequently emerge from and sit upon his shell, but would never wholly depart from it. He was handsome, highly educated, and very polite. No secret was made of his peculiar attachment to the shell in which he was born, and which had grown with him. When he became old enough to take a wife, the family's wealth soon found him a pretty young girl as his companion. Soon after the marriage, the grandmother asked the bride whether her husband left his shell at night, or lay in it by the side of his couch. The young wife replied that he left his shell on the floor, and lay by her side at night. The grandmother then told the bride to pretend that she was sleeping, and when she was sure that her husband was asleep, to jump noiselessly from the bed, seize the shell, and bring it to the grandmother's room. This plan was successfully carried out, and as the bridegroom could neither find his shell nor why it had been taken away, he lived without it, and appeared like other people.

Some happy years passed, the young wife bore sons, and all was harmonious in the house. But one day the grandmother, in the absence of her grandson, put the moldy shell out to air. The grandson unexpectedly returned, saw and recognized the shell, and at once crawled off in it to the sea, from which he never returned.

It is said one may, by urgent appeal to the gods, get a son; but the son thus gotten may be an angel or a demon.

A WIFE'S VENGEANCE

A bean-curd maker had an old mother and a pretty young wife. The wife helped her husband make the curd in a room behind the shop, and the old mother assisted in selling it at a counter extending across the front of the shop, along the quiet street. The only son of a rich merchant used to pass frequently, on his way to and from his studies, and he hoped to see the little wife. He was so impressed by her beauty that he often stopped at the counter to buy curd in the hope of getting a look at her through the door into the back room. He did this for many months, chatting sometimes with the unsuspecting husband and mother-in-law, and he came to be looked upon by them as a very honest and good customer. When the friend had become one of long standing, the three used to talk together of personal affairs.

The more the young man saw of the little wife, the more he desired her, and at last he became so jealous of her husband, whom she loved, that he determined to be rid of him. He told the husband that he was going to a distant port, in charge of goods on one of this father's junks, and that, if the husband would like to go along and take some of his goods to sell, he would give him passage, and would furnish half the money needed in the venture. The bean-curd maker thought the opportunity promising, made ready, and went on the voyage. His sales were so large that he afterward took a second journey and then a third. During the third voyage, the husband was alone with the young man on deck at night, and he was pushed overboard. The husband was a good swimmer, and swam toward the boat, but his rival repeatedly pushed him off with an oar, until he was exhausted and sank. The boat returned to its port, and the young man told the mother and wife that the man fell overboard in the night, and that, though every effort was made, he could not be saved, nor could his body be recovered.

After this the murderer continued to falsely befriend the two mourning women, being careful to manage that they should have a keen sense of their poverty and helplessness. He then sent one who appeared to be disinterested, to suggest to the two women that it would be wise for the young widow to marry some well-to-do man, who would protect her and take care of the old mother. When they had had time to think about this advice, the young man sent a formal proposal of marriage, with the promise of a monthly allowance enough to support the older woman. The little widow was anxious for the mother-in-law's welfare, and she was grateful to the rich man's son for the many favors she supposed he had done for them, so she consented to be his wife. He loved her for her beauty, and she loved him for his kindness, and they lived happily together.

After two years a son was born to them, and they were happier than ever. One day the wife reminded the husband that she had never seen all the property about their house, and suggested that, as every one else that day was seeking recreation,

A Go-Between Comes For Proposal of Marriage. The go-betweens are left and right, the one at the left is standing, the one at the right is seated at a richly carved table, probably with marble top, with mother or mother-in-law seated in center while the subject of the marriage waits, patiently. The go-between at left wears inferior grade of shoes as compared to the other with whiskers, which are seldom seen.

he should take her and the child out for a walk. He agreed, and they went out among their flower gardens and fish pools. As they stood watching the goldfish in one of the tanks, a toad hopped upon the curb, and she, in disgust, poked it off into the water with a stick. The toad swam back toward her, and she repeatedly pushed it away, till she heard her husband laugh, and suddenly looking into his face, felt sure that he was amused, not by her, but by some remembrance. She asked him to tell her why he laughed, and was not at all satisfied by his reply at her pushing the toad away was funny. Finding insistence to no avail she became angry because he would not tell her the true reason for his laughter.

He tried his best to please her, but she said that he had some memories that he did not share with her; that after she had lived with him for many years assuming that he kept nothing from her, she found that he had some memory that he would not share with her, or anyone. She made her husband miserable. Days and weeks passed, and he told her everything but the truth, but he could neither win back her smiles, nor convince her of error in her judgment. He thought about the matter again and again, and considered that she had lived happily with him for many years, and was very fond of their boy; that until the present trouble arose, she had never been other than charming, and he missed her charming ways.

After much thinking, and seeing in her no sign of yielding the point, and fearing that his happiness was at stake by silence as much as by speech, he decided to tell her all. He sat down alone with her, and said he would tell her whatever she wished

The Shoe Shop. Most Chinese wore grass sandals or light leather half boots. Here the master sits at his last while his assistant at left holds a piece of raw hide, waiting for instructions about the size required which he will neatly carve out of the hide.

to know. She began to smile so charmingly that he was encouraged to go on, and he told her that her pushing a toad away with a stick that kept swimming back toward her made him think how he had treated her first husband. She concealed her horror, and smiled and listened, and asked a few questions with winning curiosity, till she knew the whole story of the murder of her first husband.

Then, holding back the rage in her heart, she said: "The dead are dead, and we are alive; while we live let us live cheerfully." She mentioned the matter no more that day, but resumed her duties as usual, and her husband thought he had reasoned well, and that there never was so fascinating a woman as she.

That night she stabbed him in the heart while he slept. In his agony he rolled off the bed and died on the floor. Then she put on sackcloth, dishevelled her hair, girded her waist, and sitting by the dead man, awaited the morning.

When it grew late, without sound or movement in the room, her mother-in-law came to call them to breakfast. Getting no response she opened the door, and found the corpse and the

The Wheeled Chair. The "Wheeled chair" shown here in a pen drawing done in the 1870s to illustrate Miss Fielde's book on *Chinese Fairy Tales* was invented not in China but in Japan. There are several versions of the "invention" of the "ricksha" or wheeled chair, but the most interesting version has the wife of one of the U.S. Navy officers insisting on finding a better way to see the sights. Possibly, she remembered the one horse open shay or buggy pulled by a single horse hitched to two shafts, and lo, Japanese artisans picked up her thoughts on this and produced the wheeled chair. In China it was called by different names, one suggesting the bitter sweat of humans who had to pull the vehicle—which was questionable—and before long it was simply called a chin-lick-shaw, and finally evolved in the 1920s as "rickshaw" or as ricksha.

In 1949, after the Red Army occupied Shanghai, it banned the ricksha as demeaning to human labor. Actually, it was already obsolete, since one ricksha took up as much space as two bicycles, and what China now needs most is space, and millions of people, rich and poor, ride to work on a "bike," a simple invention of the late 1800s in Europe which spread to America and the world.

In the pen drawing shown here a pedestrian watches the "wheeled chair." He is pointed out because he is wearing glasses, the only illustration to include this aspect of the struggle to make tired eyes or cataracts less painful.

murderess. The magistrate was at once notified, and the woman was summoned for trial. Her own relatives, those of her two husbands, and many spectators being assembled, she told her story. Then the judge said: "You have yourself avenged the murder of your first husband; who is to avenge the murder of your second husband?" "I, myself," she answered and plunged a dagger into her heart.

THE KITCHEN GOD
(Lao Tsao Yeh)

A lithograph of the *Kitchen God* may have been presented, by Chinese friends, to Malcolm and Margaret Rosholt as they prepared to leave Shanghai in October 1937, after six years in China. The lithograph reached our home in Rosholt, Wisconsin, undamaged. We had it framed but without any clue to its illustrator or the mythology swirling around this famous god of the kitchen. Only after reading a book called *Pagoda Shadows,* written by Miss Adele M. Fielde and published in New York-Boston in 1884, did we learn more. However, the book is copyrighted not by Miss Fielde but by W.G. Courtell of Boston, probably a friend and mentor associated with Miss Fielde in Christian mission work.

Writing from Swatow (now as Shandao), Miss Fielde describes her views of the *Kitchen God* as follows:

The gods (in China) are legion. These are the great images in the large temples and odd fragments of idols in shrines; the local deities of which every village, field and mountain has its own controllers of the thunder, the rain, the harvest, and the elements; the spirits of all the dead and especially ones' ancestors. Besides these strange object (sic) and the site of every inexplicable phenomenon is worshiped. Some of the greater gods have representatives on the family, and ashes from the censor pots in the temples are frequently bright and worshiped in the houses. But whatever else may be absent from the household, the *Kitchen God* is not. He is the god of all kitchens, and no one dare set up housekeeping without his presence. He has been a god for hundreds of years, and all know the legend concerning him:

"A poor man married who soon became rich, but he discarded the wife that had brought him good luck, and as she wandered along the road, she came to a solitary hut, in which an old man sat. She told this old man her sad story and he asked her to be his wife. She lived with him in the hut and he prospered and grew rich and built a large, fine house. When the kitchen range was partially made, a man came begging to the door and she discovered in him her former husband. While she was giving him some money, her present husband approached, and the former husband hid in the kitchen range and was never seen any more. He turned into a god and is one to this day." In some families he has no image set up, and the incense sticks burned in worshipping him are stuck in the crevices of the range chimney. Many put his image in the main room of the house. His birthday is the fourteenth of the seventh month, and on that day every family worships him, each in his own house. On the fourth day of the last month of the year, when gods are supposed to go off for a ten-day holiday, a paper horse and other traveling equipment are burned for his use during his journey to make his annual report to the superior gods. A lamp is kept constantly burning during the first days of the new year to indicate that the family is waiting to welcome him whenever he returns. When children have been away from the home, after greeting their parents, they worship the *Kitchen God*. If the house mother rears fat pigs, she credits her success to the *Kitchen God's* goodwill and she makes suitable thank offerings

Kitchen God *(Lao Tsao Yeh)*

when the pigs are sold.

When the father of the family dies, and the ancestral property is divided among the sons, the eldest gets the image of the *Kitchen God*; the second gets the censor and stands before him, and others get portions of the ashes from the censor. Each then supplies what is lacking in his own religious outfit, and sets up his god, and worships it before cooking a meal in his own house.

A style of calligraphy, clear and bold, as done with a brush or stylus, by Brigadier General Wang Chih, a gift to an old friend, Malcolm Rosholt. General Wang served as a personal representative of Chiang Kai-shek attached to the staff of General Douglas MacArthur in the Philippines before Pearl Harbor, and when MacArthur withdrew to Darwin, Australia in 1942, General Wang followed him. After MacArthur's reconquest of the Philippines in 1944, Wang was assigned to other duties. In this calligraphy, Wang compares Rosholt's isolated post as a liaison officer in China to a Chinese general of the 10th Century A.D. who was probably ordered by the Emperor to put down a rebellion in Central Asia during the Northern Sung Dynasty (960-1127). The poetry follows:

A cup of unstrained wine
A home ten thousand *li* away
Victory not in sight
Homecoming unattainable
Listening to the heart-breaking melodies
   of alien flutes
Looking at the silvery frost over the land
Sleepless nights
Generals with white hair, soldiers with tears.

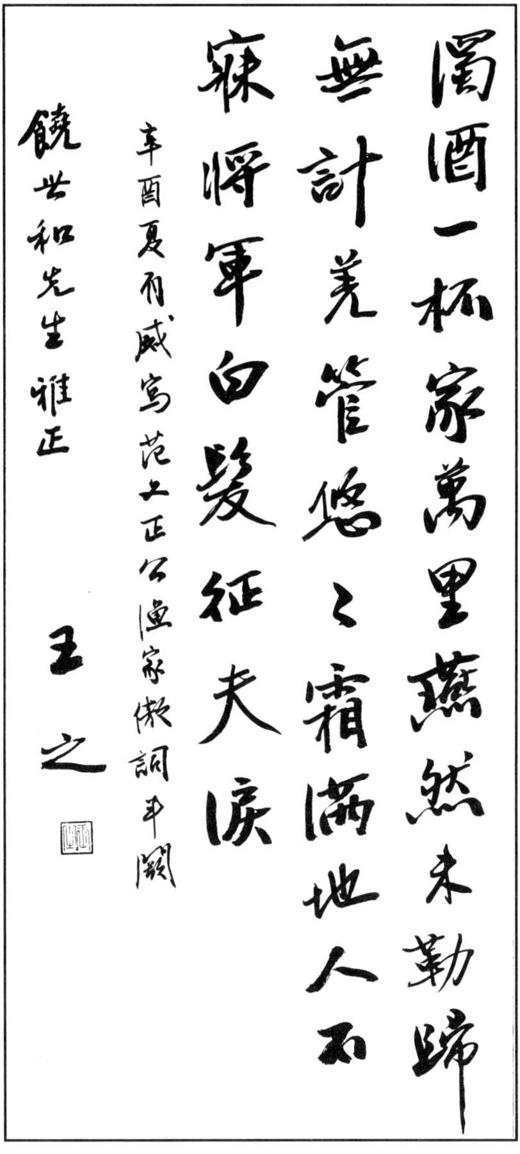
濁酒一杯家萬里燕然未勒歸
無計羌管悠悠霜滿地人不
寐將軍白髮征夫淚
辛酉夏有感寫范文正公漁家傲詞于關
饒世和先生雅正
王之

Adele M. Fielde

About Adele M. Fielde

Much that we know about the author of *Pagoda Shadows* and *Chinese Fairy Tales* seems to be summed up in an obituary which appeared in the *Seattle Post-Intelligencer* under date of February 24, 1916. The obituary, more like a life story, appeared in a three-column layout, above the fold, in a second or third section of the newspaper. The story is accompanied by a single column photo. It was one she liked and she had signed it Adele M. Fielde, and "faithfully yours." It seems she had made a big impression on the readers of the *Post-Intelligencer* in the few years since she had arrived in the city, in 1907, to live and to die. She was a feminist, and her own books attest to this by their dedications either to American women or to Chinese women, at least in the great harbor city of Swatow (now as Shandao) located about 200 miles northeast of Hong Kong.

Adele Marion Fielde had added an "e" to her name to make sure, it seems, that she was not a member of Cyrus Field family or another Field who would build a big department store in Chicago. She was born in East Rodman, New York, March 30, 1839, one of five children, four sisters and a brother. In 1860 she was graduated from Albany Normal school, which qualified her to teach grades kindergarten to eight, but there is little evidence that she did much teaching. She spent her creative energy writing or lecturing to larger audiences in and around

Boston, Massachusetts. Actually, she spent the entire period of the Civil War in the Boston area, seemingly oblivious to the life and death struggle that was then being waged by Union and Confederate forces at Gettysburg and Stone Mountain. But it was in this period when she met a man she fell in love with and he with her, namely Cyrus Chilcott, the brother of a girl Adele either shared a dormitory room with or some other arrangement. But they shared a common interest aside from their love affair: both wanted to be Christian missionaries to Southeast Asia and China.

Leaving her fiance behind for reasons never explained, Adele Fielde bought a ticket for Bangkok, Siam (now known as Thailand), on an American sailing ship, a clipper called *N.B. Palmer,* sailing out of the port of New York. There was no Suez Canal to shorten the route to Southeast Asia and the skipper sailed and tacked across the south Atlantic to reach a small settlement at the Cape of Africa, later to be called Capetown.

The writer of the *Post-Intelligencer* obit says that the voyage was "fringed by suffering and darkened by tragedy," probably a reference to events to come. At the Cape, the clipper had to tie up for a day or more while fresh water was carried on board. While this was being done, passengers went ashore to stretch their sea legs, as the saying goes, only to learn a mutiny had broken out between the officers and crew. No details seem available, but the fact is that order was restored and the *Palmer* set a course to Siam probably with a visit to the island of Ceylon (now as Sri Lanka), an island famous for its tea plantations even before the Christian era. But approaching Malaysia, the clipper was blown off course in a typhoon and the captain found a place to beach the ship on the south coast of Java (now Indonesia).

The passengers, probably, found another ship, even a Chinese junk, to sail to the Malacca Straits and on to the main port of Siam, which lies less than a hundred miles south of Bangkok.

In Bangkok, Miss Fielde was taken in hand by two Baptist missionary couples who were already established and they found an apartment or thatched-roof bungalow where she could work at her main objective, namely, to learn how to speak a Chinese dialect which was heard in the port city of Swatow. There were strong commercial ties between Swatow and Bangkok, and many Chinese agents in the import-export business. Miss Fielde was able to engage one of them to teach her the Swatow dialect of the Chinese language.

Circumstantial evidence suggests that she was not interested in learning to write or read the Chinese language, but our own admiration for her is cultural, since she seems to have been the first Christian missionary who came not only to save souls but who wanted to learn something about Chinese culture and manners.

By 1850 the King James version of the Bible seemed to have been completed, mainly by English and Scottish scholars. But, Miss Fielde wanted the people of the Swatow area to have, at least the book of Genesis, translated into the Swatow dialect. For this she went to Shanghai in the mid-1880s and spent nearly two years there writing and editing this translation, all in longhand, all, no doubt, with a steel pen or a quill, with blue ink.

Meanwhile, her fiance, Cyrus Chilcott had died either en route to Bangkok or in Hong Kong. This phase of her life is left unsolved; she never tried, it seems, to find a replacement.

At this time, that is in the 1870s, there was no system of romanization, which is to say, no way a Chinese word (tze) could be written into English, but by the 20th Century it seems that two English scholars, James Wade and Herbert Giles had worked out an acceptable system of romanization which continued to be used in dictionaries published from 1922 to 1932, and it was replaced by a new system worked out by the People's Republic of China called *pin-yin* which is usually translated as "phonetics." It is alleged that Russian grammarians assisted the Chinese scholars in this before the Chinese broke off diplomatic relations with the Soviet Union in the late 1950s.

Go Leng's Chinese name was probably Kuo or Kua Ling, or Lung, both surnames as they would be called, and both names widely known in Kwangtung province and southern Hunan.

In his pen drawings, Go Leng was probably cautioned by his sponsor not to include any woman with bound feet, a custom of physical torture for women that perhaps goes back to the Sung Dynasty.

In our rendition of *Chinese Fairy Tales* many words have been changed or eliminated to make them more understandable in contemporary society. The word "thither," for example, and the word "handmaiden" has been changed to "servant." After our baby girl was born in Shanghai, we hired a young woman to help with the baby and everyone called her "the amah."

We have also omitted a number of the fairy tales, mostly because they are uninteresting, or might be misunderstood by modern readers. We have also taken the liberty to abbreviate or change sentence structure to avoid repetition.

Fully conscious of her impending death in Seattle in October 1916, Adele M. Fielde asked her lady friends to avoid any lavish memorial service and to exclude any member of the clergy, male or female. She wanted to be cremated and her ashes spread over the waves of Lake Washington in Seattle. She left assets worth $7,500. The word "assets" is used because the word mortgage is mentioned. The $7,500 was divided equally among two sisters and two brothers called Cauldwell who each got $1,750. The estate in probate court at King's County, Washington, shows that all four Cauldwells were no blood relation to Miss Fielde, and they all lived in Hartsdale in Westchester County, New York. The name Cauldwell is usually spelled Caldwell today.

ED.NOTE—The next page, a mixture of Chinese and English text, is actually an introductory page of explanation for a book of Chinese fairy tales which are related to those recorded by Adele M. Fielde. The actual size of the wood covered book is $6^{1}/_{4}$" x $8^{3}/_{4}$" inches. The name of the author is not clear, nor can I be sure how it came into my hands, whether it was sent to me by mail or brought to me safe hand by some Chinese civilian or military officer. The dating in the lower right hand corner is July 1, 1945, done at Nanping, the provincial capital of Fujian province on the east coast of China. I was located less than a hundred miles north of Nanping at Yuanshan Wutu, headquarters of the Chinese 3rd War Area as a liaison officer and intelligence agent for the Office of Strategic Service. When I flew into Changting, an air base in south Kiangsi province on April 23, 1945, there was no station master at Changting at the time and after spending the night there I boarded a public bus to reach my destination 200 miles to the north.

Our bus stopped overnight in Nanping and I took the occasion to visit with Mr. Liu Chen-hsi, the governor of the province who lived not in Nanping but in a village nearby. He was very pleased and offered tea and cakes.

But the donor of the book of fairy tales signs his name, Chao Ch'ang-tsung. Surprisingly, the book is autographed to "Captain Rosholt," in Chinese typed *tze* (ideographs) at left of center page. Thus, the donor of the book remains unknown. It is a mystery why the artist included ten "flat peaches," which is to say, ten immortals, since the peach in Chinese mythology represents immortality and "flat" peaches are planted only once in 3,000 years.

There is no jacket on this book. The front and back covers are of wood, probably bamboo. The story line and illustrations read from right to left, the ancient method of book or scroll binding. The sub-title of the book is the *Eight Fairies Festival* which suggests it has Buddhist associations.

·一

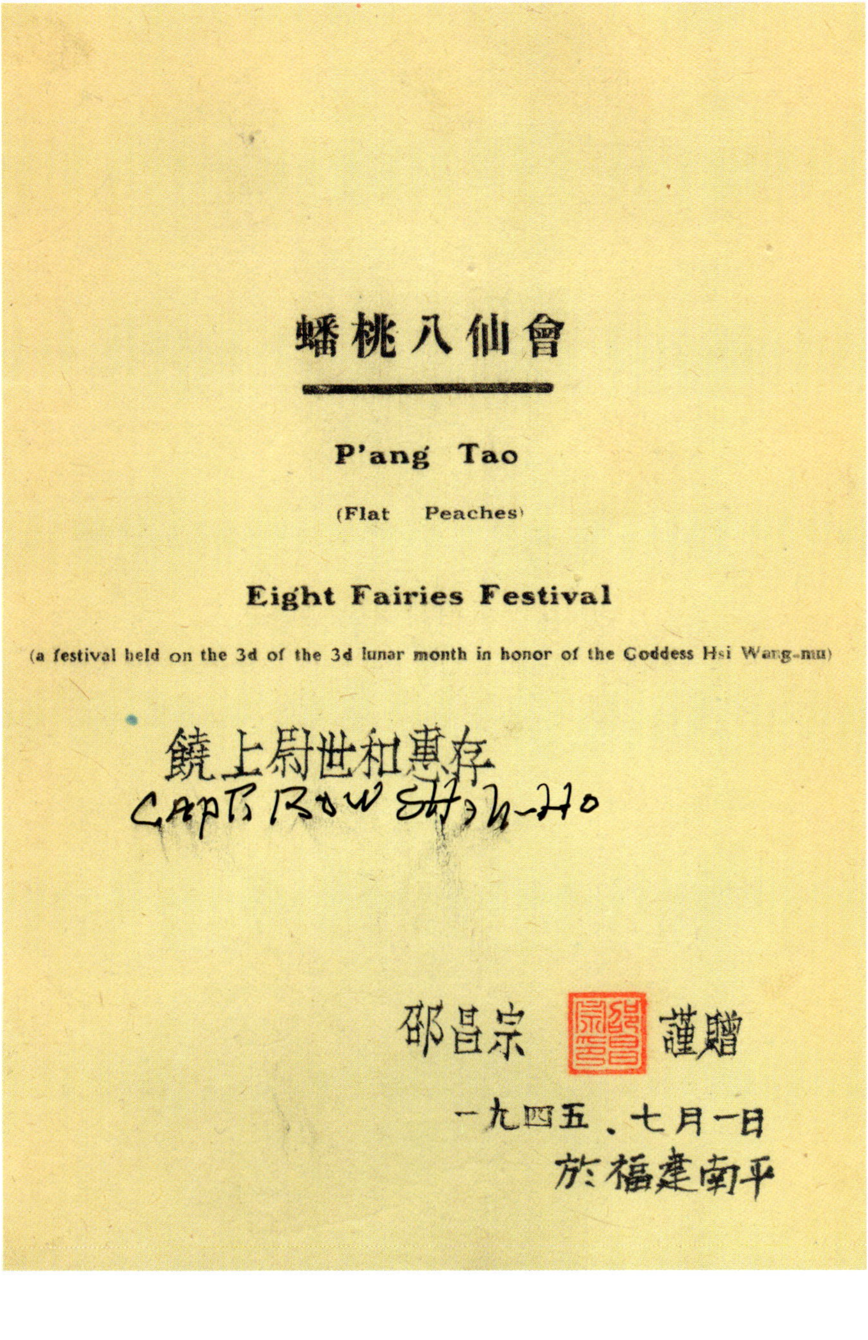
蟠桃八仙會

P'ang Tao

(Flat Peaches)

Eight Fairies Festival

(a festival held on the 3d of the 3d lunar month in honor of the Goddess Hsi Wang-mu)

饒上尉世和惠存

CAPT RAO SHIH-HO

邵昌宗 謹贈

一九四五、七月一日

於福建南平

韓鍾離

韓鐘離

HAN CHUNG LI

Han Chung Li is reputed to have lived in the Han dynasty. He was one of the searchers for immortality and was a mountain recluse. His characteristics are a bearded face and a fan to which is attached a tassel of horse hair. His fan is a magic fan with which he can revive the dead. One day in wandering about he came upon a young woman weeping at the grave of her deceased husband. Upon inquiring the reason for her presence there she replied that she was waiting for the grave to dry, for as soon as it became dry she was to marry again. Thereupon Han Chung Li began to fan the grave and instantly the husband came to life.

呂洞賓

呂洞賓

LU TUNG-PIN

Lu Tung-Pin was five feet two inches tall and at twenty still unmarried. At this time he made a journey to Lu Shan, where he met the fire dragon who presented him with a magic sword which enabled him at will to hide himself in the heavens. He met Han Chung Li and promised to do all he could to aid in the work of converting his fellow creatures to the true doctrine. In order to become worthy he was first exposed to a series of ten temptations. These being successfully overcome he was invested with supernatural powers and magic weapons, with which he traversed the empire, slaying dragons and ridding the earth of divers kinds of evils, during a period upwards of four hundred years. One time he was going about in the guise of an oil seller, intending to immortalize all who did not ask for additional weight to the quantity of oil purchased. During a whole year he met only one old lady who alone did not ask for more than was her due. So he went to her house and seeing a well in the courtyard, threw a few grains of rice into it. The water miraculously turned to wine, from the sale of which the old lady amassed great wealth. He was skillful in fencing and is always represented with his magic saber. In one hand he holds a "fly whisk" or "cloud sweeper" in the form of a horse's tail. This is the Taoist symbol of being able to fly through the air and walk upon the clouds of heaven.

李鉄拐

李鉄拐

LI T'IEN-KUAI

Li T'ien-Kuai was originally a man of good stature and fine appearance. From early youth he devoted himself to an ascetic life, living in the mountains for more than forty years. He sat on a reed mat and often forgot to eat or sleep. Being of the same surname, Li, as Lao Tzu, he besought the Great Master to descend to earth to teach him the mysteries of life. From time to time Lao Tzu appeared to Li and taught him the vanity of all earthly things. Sometimes Lao Tzu also summoned Li to interviews in his heavenly abode. It was when Li was on one of these trips with Lao Tzu to the countries of Hsi-yu that he left his material body in charge of his disciple, Lang Ling, with instructions to cremate it if he did not return within seven days. On the sixth day the disciple was called home to visit his sick mother and decided to cremate Li's perishable body. According to his original plan Li returned on the seventh day from his celestial journey, only to find that his body had been cremated and that he had no abode. On looking around he found the body of a lame beggar who had just died, and Li took this for his own double or astral body. He procured an iron stall (t'ieh knai) to support the deformed body which he had adopted as his own, and from this obtained the name of Li T'ien-kuai. He is accredited with many benevolent deeds, such as bringing to life the body of the mother of the disciple who cremated his original body. In the form of an old man he sold drugs in the market place which could cure any kind of disease, and while there he hung a gourd on the wall of the house. Into this gourd he retired at night, going out the following day to attend to his sales. He preferred to associate with the poor and needy thus acquiring a reputation for benevolence. The characteristic of this Immortal is the ill shaped body of a beggar, who carries an iron staff in his hand, and a gourd on his back.

曹國舅

曹國舅

TSAO KUO CHIU

Tsao Kuo Chiu was a younger brother of the Empress Jen Taung. He was a man of exemplary character who attempted to persuade his dissolute brother to lead a good life. He said to his brother, "You may escape the penalty of the law, but you can never elude the net of heaven which is invisible but always present." He gave all his money to the poor and retreated to the mountains where he lived as a recluse. He was visited by Chung Li and Lu T'ung Pin with whom he conversed about spiritual matters. He said, "I am engaged in studying the Way." "What Way and where is it?" they asked. He pointed to the sky. "Where is the sky," they went on. He pointed to his heart. The two visitors smiled and said, "The heart is the sky and the sky is the Way: understand the origin of things." Then they gave him a recipe for perfection to enable him to take his place among the perfect ones. In a few days he reached this condition. He became one of the eight immortals because the other seven who occupied the eight grottoes in upper spheres wished to see the eighth inhabited and nominated him because his disposition resembled that of a genie. His characteristics are that he is dressed in official robes, wears an official hat, and carries in his right hand a tablet signifying his rank and his right to imperial audience.

何仙姑

七

何仙姑

HO HSIEN KU

Ho Hsien Ku. An immortal represented as a maiden holding in her hand a magic lotus blossom, the flower of open heartedness or peach of immortality. At her birth six hairs were found growing on the crown of her head and it is said that she never had any more; the pictures represent her with a full head of hair. She elected to live on "mother of pearl" mountain. In a dream she saw a spirit who ordered her to powder and eat one of these pearl stones from the mountain by doing which she could acquire both agility and immortality. She complied with this injunction and also vowed herself to a life of virginity. Her days were thenceforth passed in floating from peak to peak, bringing at night to her mother the fruits she collected on the mountain. She gradually found that she had no need to eat in order to live. Her fame having reached the ears of the empress, she was invited to court, but while journeying thither, suddenly disappeared from mortal view and became an immortal.

張果老

一

張果老

CHANG KUO LAO

Chang Kuo Lao. The type or emblem of an old man. At first he was a hermit. He was frequently invited to court by the emperors but he persistently refused to go. At last, pressed once more by Empress Wu he consented to leave his retreat, but was struck down at the gate of the temple. His body began to decay and to be eaten by worms, when lo! he was seen again, alive and well, on the mountains. He rode on a white mule which carried him thousands of miles in a day and which when the journey was finished, he folded up like a sheet of paper and put away in his wallet. When he again required its services he had only to spurt water upon the packet from his mouth and the animal at once assumed its proper shape. At all times he performed wonderful feats of necromancy. He is usually seen mounted on a white mule, sometimes facing its head sometimes its tail. He carries a phoenix feather or a peach of immortality. He entertained the emperors with a variety of magical tricks, such as rendering himself invisible, drinking a cup of aconite, and felling birds or flowers by pointing at them. A picture of Chang Kuo Lao sitting on a donkey and offering a descendant to a newly married couple is often found in the nuptial chamber.

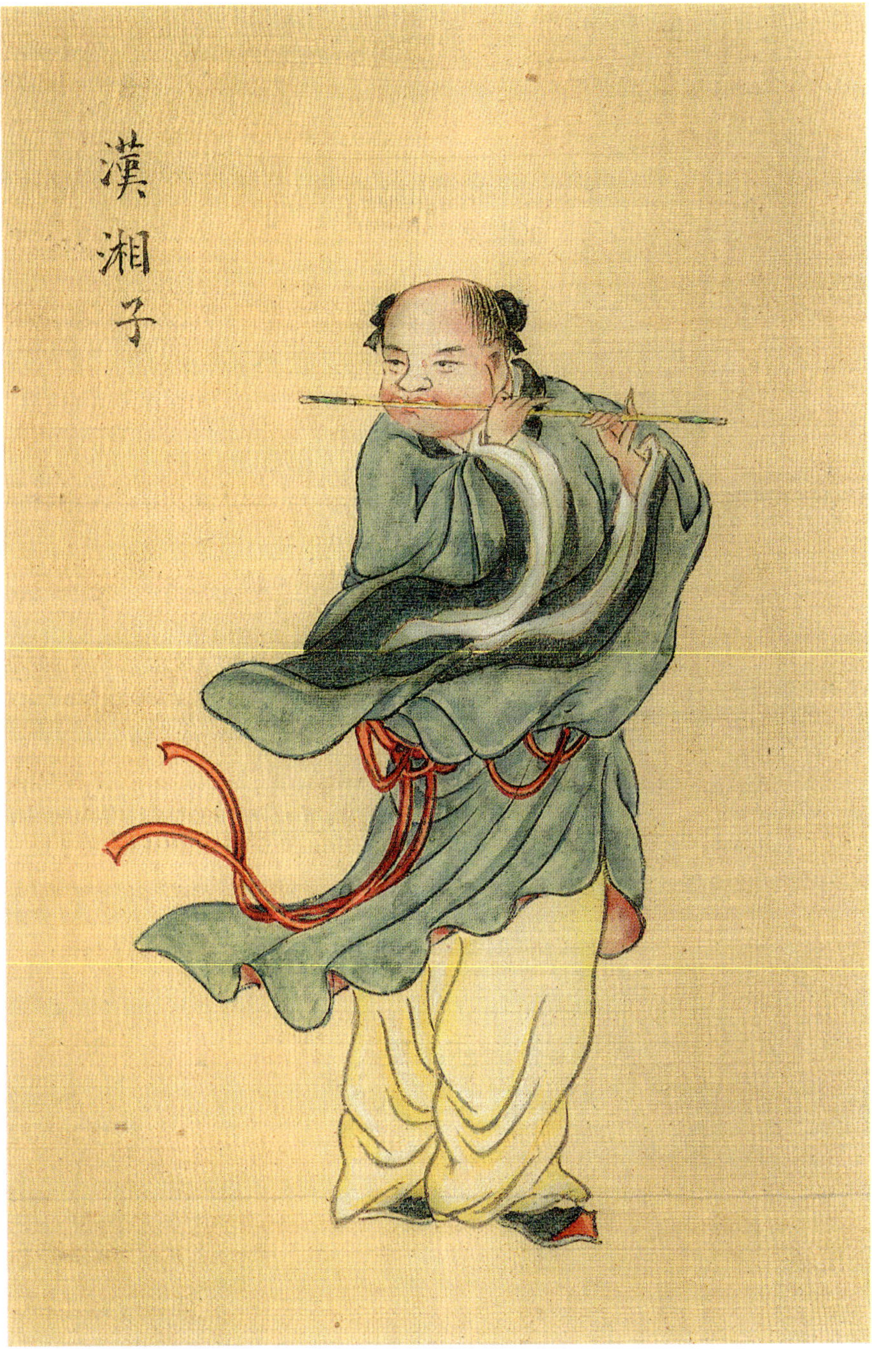
漢湘子

漢湘子

HAN HSIANG TZU

Han Hsiang Tzu was entrusted to his uncle to be educated and prepared for public examinations. His uncle was a strenuous opponent of all forms of magic. Contrary to the wishes of his uncle, the youth did not study for the public examinations but instead became a convert of Lu Tung Pin. He wished to be able to produce good wine without the use of any grain and also to be able to cause flowers to bloom instantaneously. When the uncle expressed doubt as to his being able to defy the laws of nature, Han Hsiang Tzu put a little earth under a basin and upon lifting it disclosed two flowers on the leaves of which were written in gold characters a poem, two lines of seven characters each. The characteristic of Han Hsiang Tzu is a gourd shaped basket full of the peaches of immortality and held in the two hands, and playing a flute. Sometimes he is also represented holding a basket of flowers. He earned his livelihood by singing in the streets.

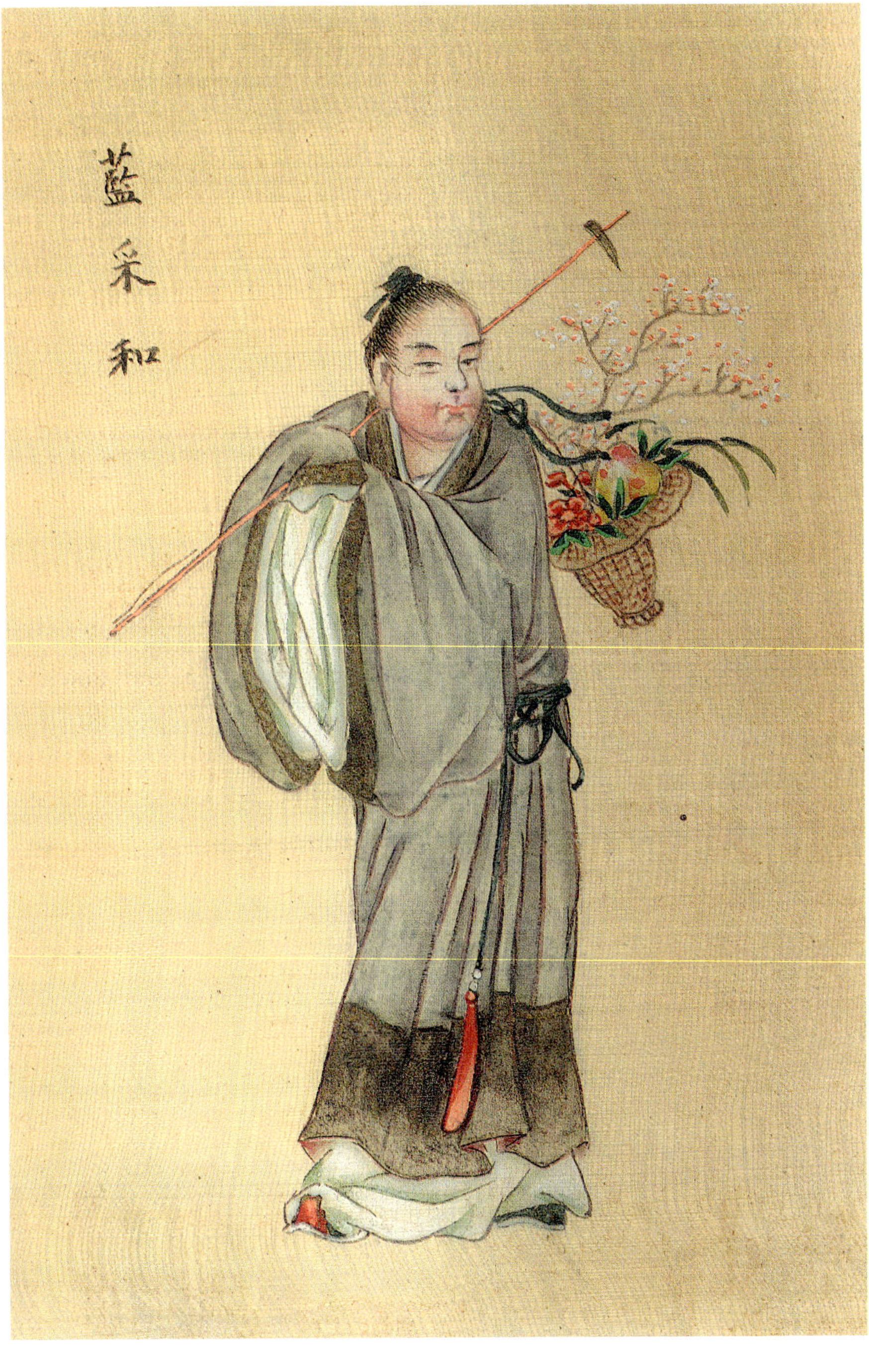
藍采和

七

藍采和

LAN TSAI HO

Lan Tsai Ho, is always represented as a youth bearing a basket of fruits. There has been much dispute as to the sex of this personage. Some state that Lan was a female. She wandered abroad in a tattered blue gown held by a black wooden belt, with one foot shoeless, wearing in summer an undergarment of wadded material and in winter sleeping on the snow, her breath rising in a brilliant cloud like steam from a boiling cauldron. When given money she either strung it on a cord and waved it to the time of her song or scattered it on the ground for the poor to pick up. One day she was found to have become intoxicated and while in that state disappeared on a cloud having thrown down to earth her shoe, robe, belt, and castanets.

南極星君

•ノ

老壽星

LAO SHOU HSING
(The Star of Longevity)

There are two stories in connection with Lao Shou Hsing. The first Feng K'an Wang Pen Shih Chi, (Feng Shan Shu Number 6 folio 15) states that the old gentleman with white beard and gnarled staff represents the "South Pole Old Man Star." When people are able to get a vision of this star the whole world is at peace. Temples have been built to this star in order to secure long life and prosperity.

The same article about Lao Shou Hsing says that when the two signs of the Zodiac Chiao and K'ang reach the position of Ch'en in their celestial journey (which is usually during the 3rd Moon or in April) they are called Shou Hsing, or The Star of Longevity. The reason for this is that these signs show up during the 3rd Moon (or usually April) when the Spring air brings forth renewed activity among all kinds of life. As the Spring air advances all living creatures and plants grow in orderly sequence and nothing is harmed. These facts show that altho' life has been dormant in some ways during the long winter months, in fact life is never extinguished. Therefore, The Star of Longevity is represented as an old man with white beard carrying a gnarled staff. He has a smile on his face as if he is able to tell the world that life goes on and on for eternity.

Note. The Chiao sign of the Zodiac appears in the heavens at the time of Ch'ing Ming (Pure Brightness) Festival, which usually occurs about the 5th or 6th of April at 12:24 midnight.

The K'ang sign of the Zodiac may be seen at 12:16 midnight during the Ku Yu (Grain Rain) Festival, which usually occurs on or about the 20th or 21st of April.

西王母

西王母

HSI WANG-MU
(King's Mother of the West)

Hsi Wang-mu is an ancient fairy princess. Her maiden surname is Yang and her name is Hui, alias Wan-chin. She is said to dwell on the beach of Swift Sands, in the Western Frontier, to have troops of fairies and genii under her command.

Once Emperor Hsia Hou-i, of Hsia Dynasty (2205-1766 B.C.), who was a famous archer, asked for elixir of immortality from Hsi Wang-mu, but Sh'ang E, a beautiful lady, stole the elixir and fled with it to the moon, where she was changed into a frog.

Later Emperor Chou Mu-wang, of Chou Dynasty (1122-255 B.C.), was very much interested in fairies. He paid a call on Wang-mu at Yao Ch'ih, a pool in fairyland in the country of Hsi Wang-mu.

Wang-mu is well-known in planting P'ang Tao, flat peaches, that bear fruits once every 3,000 years. It is said that she bestowed four pieces P'ang Tao on Emperor Han Wu-ti, of the Han Dynasty (206 B.C.-220 A.D.). Its taste was so sweet and delicious that Tung Fang-shuo, a minister of Wu-ti, stole and ate the peaches. Subsequently when the Eastern Frontier Tribes presented a dwarf to Wu-ti, the dwarf, upon meeting Fang-shuo, told the Emperor that Tung was a bad egg, having had three times stolen Wang-mu's peaches.

Ornamental flint stone kit (slightly reduced), with embossed silver work showing two dragons facing each other, claws extended and grasping for control of ball in center, probably representing the Earth. It can be assumed that every Mongol calvary detachment, in their campaigns to conquer north China and central Asia in the Yuan Dynasty, carried a larger kit with steel point and piece of quartz to start a fire. This ancient token was purchased in 1935 by Rosholt at an antique shop in Inner Mongolia.

HUNAN
KIANGSI
114
Lo-ch'ang
Jen-hua
Nan-hsiung
Wu Shui
Cheng Shui
Shih-hsing
Ch'ü-chiang
SHAO-KUAN
Ju-yüan
Lien-hsien
Lien-nan(San-chiang)
-shan
g-ho)
Yang-shan
SHAO-KUAN C. C.
Lien Chiang
Lien-
Weng-yüan
(Lung-hsien)
Ying-te
Pei Chiang
Hsin-feng
Huai-chi
HSIN-FENG
CHIANG
Fo-kang
(Shih-chiao)
Lung-men
Ch'ing-yüan
Sui Chiang
Kuang-ning
(Nan-chieh)
Ts'ung-hua
HUI-YA
KUANG-CHOU
Hua-hsien
(Hsin-hua)
SHIH
Ssu-hui
ING C. C.
Tseng-ch'eng
Ho-k'ou
San-shui
(Hsi-nan)
Po-lo
Kao-yao
O-CH'ING
FO-SHAN
Nan-hai
CANTON
Hui-yang
HUI-CH
Tung-kuan
P'an-yü
(Shih-ch'iao)
Shun-te
(Ta-liang)
Kao-ho
(Sha-p'ing)
ng
Pao-an
(Shen-chen)
CHIANG-MEN
Hsin-hui
Chung-shan
(Shih-ch'i-chen)
HONG KONG
(U.K.)
K'ai-p'ing
(San-pu)
FO-SHAN C. C.
T'an Chiang
Kowloon
Victoria
Chu-hai
(Hsiang-chou)
T'ai-shan
Tou-men
En-p'ing
Macao
MACAO
(PORT.)